MW01250964

Tisarian's Treasure

By J.M. Martin

A HEROIC FANTASY NOVELLA
Set in the World of Khaladune

The original version of "Tisarian's Treasure" was printed as a short story in *Sails & Sorcery: Tales of Nautical Fantasy*, published 2007 by Fantasist Enterprises and edited by W.H. Horner.

Check out *Sails & Sorcery* and the Fantasist Enterprises web site for more great stories.

ISBN-13: 978-1466255388 (pbk.)
ISBN-10: 1466255382 (pbk.)

Written by J.M. Martin.
Interior artist Julie Dillon.
Cover artist Peter Ortiz.
Copyedited by Sara Reinke.

Visit the author's web site:
http://www.ranting-and-raven.blogspot.com

ACKNOWLEDGMENTS

Special thanks to several folks for their support of my writing efforts. Foremost, Tracy, for your patience and for telling me (more than once) to just "get off your ass and do it."

Thanks must also go to Eric Wolfe for personifying Tisarian and breathing him to life, and to fellow world-maker, Tone Parsons, without whom Khaladune would not be near as awesome.

To my fellow creative soldiers-in-arms, the fearless company scrawled in the annals of legend as the Writers of the Storm: Kenny Soward, Johnny "Beorn" Seabolt, David "The Golden God" Dalglish, Kate Martin, Steven E. Schend, Sara Reinke, Bill "Black Wolf" Danner, and Jon Sprunk (thanks for the cover blurb, my friend)—if you enjoy this tale, please check out Jon's, as well.

Big ups to W.H. Horner for accepting and publishing the original "Tisarian's Treasure," and to the amazing talents of interior artist Julie Dillon and cover artist Peter Ortiz, for lending their artistic efforts to my vision.

Last but not least, thank you, David Gemmell, wherever you are. Here, in this mortal realm at least, Your Legend Lives On.

TISARIAN'S TREASURE

An Uncharted Island
The West Tradesea
Keeper's Age (KA) 2142

WE STOOD—MOST OF US, THAT IS—on a pebble shore, transfixed each in his or her own combination of horror and dismay. We watched it burn. Little more than black shapes of so much flotsam along the mist-choked island coast; that was the doom of the *Decimus*, our gallant caravel. We were soaked, frightened, some wounded to various extents, and I knew it wasn't the fate of the ship that concerned us so much as our own.

Doing my best to penetrate the black smoke and fog, I squinted beyond the burning wreckage. Whether it was my eyes or my panicked mind that illumined the silhouette, I cannot say, but there it came, a tall black three-masted galleon, cleaving the choppy black sea. On her deck, I knew, stood a maligned figure, scowling and ferocious, discerning the ruin of the *Decimus* with a critical eye.

Captain Thadieus Drake, bane of the West Tradesea.

He would not be fooled by our ploy. I had voiced as much, echoing despicable Oberon Teag, for the both of us, much as I reviled to say it, had something in common. We most certainly did, for we'd been pressed under the employ of that black-hearted devil, though only one of us had taken to it eagerly.

"We should make inland," murmured Teag, an edge of desperation to his voice. "'Be comin' on, 'e will, wi'v a vengeance after he sorts it out, I daresay."

"What of the boat?" asked the cabin boy—Dominy I believe his name.

"To th' hells wi' th' boat! What about Cap'n Bellows?" shouted Boatswain Marshall, who, like me, seemed to have been immersed in a cauldron of blood, none of it our own. His voice, much too loud for anyone's tastes, caromed off the cliffs above us. We winced as his echo rolled out to sea, and that's how I knew they suspected, as I did, that our ordeals were far from over.

I noticed—since he was standing next to me—the Albiyan called Hamish impart a dark scowl to the boatswain, then glare out to sea. A bull-necked freebooter with a tow-headed shock of knife-cut hair, he stood carapaced in ash-coated, gore-smeared iron and leather, and, as I'd witnessed recently, was rather versed in the issue of bloodletting. My inquiries had led me to find he was once an officer in the Albiyan navy, forced into early retirement, discharged dishonorably it was said, but I could gather nothing more. Considering the man's usual manner, I was content to leave my curiosity unsated.

Eight crewmembers of the erstwhile *Decimus* had made it to shore in the ship's boat. This desperate flight came after Lieutenant Jeric Hensley, the ship's first mate, gave the order to fire the already-sinking caravel. Unfortunately, the pirate Thadieus Drake and his crew aboard the *skein*-galleon, the *Tatterdemalion*, slithered out of a secluded inlet as we skimmed the coast of an island we believed was destined to make us wealthy beyond our imaginings. Well, perhaps not all of us; one or two skeptics unwittingly found themselves aboard. But skeptic or no, all of us to a man—one being a lady actually—felt our blood cool in our veins at the sight of that dreaded black flag with its laughing crimson skull.

The chase had been brief. Drake was in no mood to bandy words. I was familiar enough with the *Tatterdemalion*, having been aboard her for the better part of three months, to know we stood nary a chance.

Dark magic sailed her, and she bore fourteen culverins to each side, two sliding falconets at the bow, another three pointed aft, a long nine for bow or stern, and Drake at her helm. His voice thundered across the dark water: "Run 'em out, and send 'em all to the Nine!"

The Nine hells, that is.

I'd like to say the fight was a valiant one, but how does the dove fare beneath the goshawk? Of course, that's putting it poetically somewhat. The *Tatterdemalion* blew the crew of the *Decimus* to who-knows-what-level-of-hell; I suppose a deep, black, watery, dismal one. I'm certain there's a name for it, but it eludes me, which is precisely what those of us who remained alive hoped we'd done. Eluded Thadieus Drake.

Among those in flight was the unconscious captain, Laurens Bellows, freed of the anguish of witnessing his ship's consignment to the deep by a mess of shrapnel, and three of his crew: his first mate, Lieutenant Jeric Hensley, fair, moderate, the very paragon of a naval officer; Boatswain Bartholomew Marshall, an ill-tempered chap with a thick walrus mustache who was blind in one eye from a collision with a loose jib in his earlier sailing days and young Master Dominy, a fledgling cabin boy of no more than ten. Also standing on the shore, the aforementioned Hamish, a mercenary bounty hunter and his captive, Oberon Teag, upon whom this whole affair seemed to hinge, damn him, and a secret passenger, an intriguing Anturian who'd only deigned to share her first name, Katalin. Oh, and myself.

"Doctor Mallory? Haver look, will ye?"

Alexandre Mallory, that's me. A promising young doctor, born of an influential Berdainese family, studied at Nantyrr in Thansia, and just one year ago awarded my chirurgeon's license along with the Royal Doctorial Marque.

Lieutenant Hensley peered up from where he kneeled next to the captain, who lay pale and sodden on the wet stones. All faces turned to me.

"Of course," I replied.

"Now's not bein' the best time," interrupted the towering Hamish, a mailed glove still gripping his heavy claymore, the other heavily laid suddenly upon my shoulder. "We'd best get ourselves from sight."

"Aye, but th' boy's got a point. They'll see th' boat," the boatswain pointed out, indicating the sloop where it pitched in the shallow surf.

"We move it, then. Behind yon boulders. Let's go." The last utterance was growled at Oberon Teag along with a rough shove in the boat's direction. The boatswain, the bounty hunter, and the glaring prisoner all grasped the gunwales and heaved.

"Some help, Doctor?" Marshall implored.

I nodded, pulling my leathern chirurgeon's satchel's shoulder strap over my head and setting it down. I moved alongside Teag and grabbed hold of the boat, noticing the stitch-marked scar running along the anterior of the man's forearm—my handiwork. The stitching, that is; not the lesion that had furrowed his arm some months agone.

"Heave!" called Hamish, and together the four of us managed to drag the ship's boat out of the surf several paces up the beach.

I'd venture to guess we were more than a good dozen staggering steps inland, at least, when we heard that terrible, recurring thump, a noise strikingly familiar to the sailor's ear. A distant medium-pitched hiss suddenly became a keening wail.

Teag's stubbly chin dropped open. "Bugger this," he said, then broke away into a sprint. His wide-set, heavy-lidded eyes, short nose, and long upper lip had always conveyed a chelonian air in my mind, strangely reminding me of a leatherback turtle; yet, ever swift and fleet of foot, the man was far from turtle-like in his actions. Hamish, the Albiyan, dashed after him with a rumbling snarl.

Two of its bearers having run off, the ship's boat thudded to the ground. I looked to the boatswain, whose head swiveled skyward, wide brow furrowed.

From several spans away, Lieutenant Hensley called for us to take cover an eye's blink before the beach around us and the cliffs above rained shards of rock and dust. We were too late. I pictured Drake grinning through his spyglass, watching amusedly as his eighteen-pounders spit bedlam and fear upon us.

I dropped to my hands and knees and pressed against the side of the longboat, knowing it made flimsy protection but unable to do otherwise. The boatswain darted off toward the remainder of the crew, all in the wake of Teag and the Albiyan bounty hunter, who chased his fleeing prisoner toward the sheer cliffs some long yards distant.

A cannonball slammed the shoreline, and jets of gravel and sea spray pelted me. I would have clutched my knees, clenched my eyes, and prayed to the gods of my fathers there and then if it were not for an odd sight suddenly commanding my interest.

Thin and long-limbed, auburn hair pulled loosely back so that wet-dark ringlets framed her freckled face, Katalin walked toward the sea. Her hazel eyes fixed to mine with an undisturbed gaze as she bent down and retrieved my satchel from where it lay, while the *Tatterdemalion's* guns continued to powder the coast.

Pebbles and earth splattered us both as she approached in a casual woman's gait. She smiled and extended my leather bag down to me. "You will need this soon, Doctor."

How strange it seemed, that smile, barely crooked white teeth and dimpled cheeks displayed in a poise and surety amidst all the chaos. She offered her hand, as well. "You and I have nothing to fear. Leastways not yet. But we do need to leave the beach. Come."

I don't recall taking the satchel from her, but I do recall taking her hand, soft and long-boned like the rest of her, and feeling an immediate sense of calm and confidence. A strange feeling, that. I didn't know anything about Katalin then, but in that moment I became her thrall.

We dashed toward the others, and though the beach exploded thrice more behind us, we caught up to Lieutenant Hensley and young Dominy as they grappled with the burden of their inert captain. The first mate yelled to Boatswain Marshall to lend a hand and the man rushed to grab the captain's ankles from the cabin boy. I bit my tongue, knowing it unwise to jostle the wounded captain, but realizing, too, that Drake robbed us of any choice to the contrary.

"O'er here!" graveled the Albiyan in a deep bellow. He pointed after Teag, who was already scrambling around a corner in the cliff face.

We hurried over some shallow dunes, weaving amid patches of tall silt grass, into a cleft of sorts where a talus slope of earth ramped sharply upward, yet not so sharp as to be insurmountable. We scrabbled in bits of scree, but enough rocky outcrops were fixed to give purchase for a labored ascent, and I managed to scale to the high ground with little more than scuffed palms and a few other minor scrapes—a small price to pay for the corner we'd turned, removing us from the *Tatterdemalion's* barrage. The men hefting the motionless captain were the last to make it up. I saw, too, that Hamish had Oberon Teag well in hand, hard words shared between them.

The first mate and the boatswain plunked down beside the captain, and even young Dominy looked belabored, using his neck rag to wipe sweat from his brow. I bent, hands to knees, and took a breather, as well.

Lieutenant Hensley's voice snapped my attention from watching Katalin, who stood nearby, bosom rising and falling, accentuated by her tight-laced bodice. "We shan't tarry here, as I'm expecting Drake'll be making for land even now, but if'n ye please, Doctor?"

"Certainly," I replied, rather embarrassed, fearing having been caught with a roving eye in that improper moment. "Of course."

I moved to the unconscious Captain Bellows and went to a knee, placing the side of my face near his colorless lips. I could not tell if his breath or the sea air barely draped my cheek. I snaked two fingertips inside his high collar, placing them on his upper neck aside the distinct protrusion of his larynx. After a moment's hesitation, I found it; his pulse coursed weakly in the *carotis arturiolis*, a vital conduit for passage of blood and humors to the brain.

"His pulse is faint, his breathing labored," I said to Hensley. "I fear I cannot help him unless I treat him straightaway, Lieutenant."

"Then we need to find shelter, a place to hide—"

"Every time he's moved you risk more damage," I interrupted. "I need to treat him here, right now. For all I know, the damage is already beyond my ability to repair."

The first mate met my gaze and chewed the inside of his lip, unsure how to answer. He didn't need to voice his fear. The explosions on the beach had stopped and, even now, Drake and his roughest cutthroats likely rowed their way to shore. I recollected the evil eyes and ugly face of Aubrid the Myg Rothan, the one they called the Albatross, and I shivered; I'd witnessed his savage pleasures firsthand and Drake would most certainly have picked him as part of the landing party.

"That bein' the case, hardly matters if we move him some more," called out Teag from where he stood next to the towering Albiyan.

Everyone watched expectantly. Lieutenant Hensley's jaw muscles clenched, then he sighed through his nose. His brown-eyed gaze met mine. "I'm loath to admit, but he's right. We need to keep moving. The captain would understand."

"Aye." Boatswain Marshall bobbed his head.

Prudence dictated our actions, and though my years of training urged further contention on the captain's behalf, I choked it down and nodded. We stood, and both Hensley and Marshall took up the motionless Bellows, his pallor that of a dead man's, and we moved hastily landward.

On the terrace, we traversed a short rock-strewn incline to a tangled mass of verdant, sharp-leafed palms, interspersed with other yellow-barked trees dangling thick strands of moss. The jungle extended both ways as far as we could tell, and away from the ocean I became aware of the heat of the day with the sun beating down from where it hung overhead in the cloudless blue. The sounds of the sea, too, faded away and instead the jungle called out; from within its foliage I could hear a diversity of tropical birds as they screeched and tittered.

The sea spray on my skin had since turned to sweat, and I found my gaze once more on Katalin, thanks to her décolleté garment. She stood quite near to me as we surveyed the jungle, sweating prettily, rivulets coursing down her exposed collarbone and over the tops of her breasts. I became aware that I wasn't the only one casting a lascivious eye. Oberon Teag's weathered face shared a brown-toothed smile, as if we were somehow bonded by virtue of maleness. I frowned and looked away.

"Now where to?" the boatswain asked, his craggy features made all the more rough as he frowned and re-adjusted his grip on the captain.

"If shelter's our aim, seems not much choice but in," answered Hamish with a jerk of his head, aiming his large chin at the trees.

Hensley peered with a grim eye at the jungle. His face dripped sweat, chest rising and falling, and mimicking Boatswain Marshall he, too, shifted the captain's weight.

As the first mate chewed on the decision, I chanced another glance at Katalin. It interested me to see her expression drained of all color as her gaze fell into some middle distance between Boatswain Marshall and herself. I touched her arm lightly. "Are you well, m'lady?" I asked, feeling genuine concern.

She paused in answering for such a while that I suspected she was in some sort of trance-like state, then her eyelids fluttered. Katalin suspired expressively, and her face turned in my direction. She leaned close. Something rippled in my chest as she did so. "For whatever good it's worth," she said in low tones meant for my ears only, "don't let the boatswain near the water."

"Excuse me, m'lady?"

"Why I'm telling you this, I know not. My warnings fail to ever make a difference, but I'm telling you, Doctor, I've seen that man's end. It's not a good one...though they rarely are."

"I don't quite follow."

"No, I shouldn't think you would," she responded.

Confusion must have clearly etched itself on my face during our exchange, I'm sure, whereas the first mate evidently came to a decision, barked something terse, and the group began moving into the trees.

"Come, Doctor," Katalin said softly as she turned from me and followed after them.

If I felt trepidation before stepping into the shadows of the island forest, a few strides into its depths, my eyes struggled to pierce the brooding darkness, and those feelings of foreboding turned to pure dread. The gravity of our predicament dawned on me. We no longer had a ship or a way to sail from this unmapped island, while walking into some nameless jungle where death lay in wait for fools as victims. We had no food, no water, and no clear destination in mind, lugging our unconscious ship's captain and, of course, yes, the most feared pirate from Harrathun's Channel to the West Tradesea came hard on our heels with a band of cutthroats and freebooters at his beck and call.

"What is it precisely that we're doing here?" I called ahead to the first mate. "I mean, where exactly are we *going?*"

"Your guess be good as mine," Hensley replied. "I don't know where we're going, Doctor, but we must needs find shelter for Captain Bellows. I don't know if we'll elude that vulture Drake, so we can only pray for a defensible position—or a miracle."

So we continued.

The jungle had no trails to speak of, so at Hensley's behest Hamish moved to the fore and began using his claymore to scythe away at the tangled networks of vines, bushes, and small trees. His weapon proved no substitute for a machete, and we were often forced to turn back and find an alternative course. Every time we did so I feared running into our pursuers. If someone with even a mote of tracking experience were among Drake's landing party, it would be a simple matter to uncover the broken limbs and trampled underbrush of our passage.

Despite my fears, we remained undiscovered, through what felt like leagues of foliage and webs of vines, often over treacherous footing, amidst spiders, snakes, some form of large rodent-like creature, and birds of every cry and color I could imagine. We finally came upon a clearing where grew a variety of flowers and weeds, and here we paused to rest.

I immediately saw to the poor captain, who'd remained clinging to life throughout the long day. His flesh was cold and bloodless, his pupils enlarged so that no evidence of his slate-gray eyes could be found. I palpated his wounds and was sorely dismayed to find part of his head above the ear puffed out and slick with blood. With a finger, I probed beneath the split skin to find his skull had all the fragility of a cracked bird's egg. Frowning, I removed some instruments from my chirurgeon's satchel. "I need water," I said softly to Hensley.

"He needs water," said the first mate, past me to the others.

"We all do," Oberon Teag dryly grated in response.

The Albiyan shoved rudely past Teag, evidently still in a foul way since having to misuse his weapon earlier in the day, and approached. "Here. A full skin," he said, taking out a waterskin from a weathered leather pouch at his left hip.

I accepted it with a nod of thanks and used the water to clean blood from the captain's scalp. Teag murmured something about "water damn wasted," obtaining several hard glares.

Once the blood was somewhat washed away, I drew what fluid I could with a cannula and proceeded to suture the wound with flax and bandage his head with linen. It was the only treatment I could offer, and I harbored little hope. In a fog of exhaustion I conveyed as much to Lieutenant Hensley, with the boatswain and cabin boy looking on. Hensley merely nodded and tried pouring some of the water into the captain's mouth, but it dribbled out. After another try, the first mate shook his head and handed the skin back to Hamish with a word of thanks.

The Albiyan passed the skin around with a scrutinizing eye to ensure everyone took a liberal amount, then we all sat resting in morose silence for a spell.

"The day's fading," Hensley finally said. "No sense moving the captain more today. We'll rest here for the night."

No one issued a better idea and, in truth, all seemed quite leaden. Myself, I could no longer walk without my knees buckling, and Teag appeared already asleep, slouched at the base of a nearby tree. I looked to Katalin, who merely sat hugging her knees and gazing once more into that mysterious middle distance. Hensley, Marshall, and Hamish agreed to a watch order, then the lieutenant told the rest of us to get what sleep we could.

A chilly mist enshrouded us as night fell. I lay curled on a flat rock, fading in and out of awareness for the first hour or two, unable to sleep, fretting and fighting the urge to start at every little night noise. In time, I rose to make relief, and managed to quietly find my way to a nearby tree, whereupon I heard whispering: "We've got Teag and his bloody map, so we sail the course."

"Aye, 'cept what's the point, eh? Treasure's no good if we can't hie ourselves gone from this wretched place. I say we parlay wiv' Drake 'n strike a deal."

The first voice was Lieutenant Hensley's, the other Boatswain Marshall's. "Drake's got no honor," replied Hensley. "Nothing would stop him from killing every one of us and just taking Teag's map."

"You see dis map, den? 'Ow we know it even exists?"

"I haven't seen it, but the Albiyan says Teag has it."

"How come the Albiyan don't have it hisself? Why's 'e lettin' that rascal keep it? An' so if we do find this thing, we still be stuck on the island, so what then, eh?"

If included in the exchange, I could bear out the details for them. I knew how the 'rascal' managed to keep it in his possession. But Marshall had a point. Treasure or no, we were undeniably fixed in an ill predicament.

"Eavesdropping, Doctor?" a voice whispered in my ear. My startlement must have been evident even in the dark, for Katalin continued by softly saying, "Be at ease. It matters naught to me. I eavesdrop all the time, usually in spite of myself."

Her hand touched my shoulder, her sudden presence stirring my senses, but I managed to control myself passably. "You have a look about you sometimes," I whispered, "as if seeing something that's not there. Is…is that it?"

The moon shined down from high above, filtering through the leaves, limning her black shadow in an eerie white glow. She imparted a brief smile, I could see, but a flickering thing, gone too soon.

"You *do* see things, m'lady." I pressed, leaning in, carefully keeping my voice low, our faces mere inches apart. She seemed a ghost amid the grotesque silhouettes, and my pulse quickened even more. "What did you mean when you said not to let the boatswain near the water?"

"I've learned, Doctor…" She spoke hesitatingly. "I've learned there's no sense in it, telling you what I see. It changes nothing. All comes to pass, whither I endeavor to stave it off or no, but I can tell you this: you will be there, at the end; you, me, the boy…and *Drake*. I foresaw it months ago. It's why I booked passage on the *Decimus*.

"'Tis a strange thing, Doctor. Through the years I've learned it leads, I follow, and that's how it's been. Now, my destiny lies ahead of us. Yours, too."

"You have me at a loss," I said, feeling flushed as I looked at her. What hold this lady had on me! I could not recollect feeling so riveted to another woman in all my days.

She returned my gaze then, a deep stare, piercing, unlike her usual distant tendency. Her eyes reflected moonlight and cut a path into my soul, halting my very breath.

Katalin reached up, putting her hand against the side of my face. It was uncommonly cool. "Don't be startled," she said.

"What do you—"

Her bare forearm changed, and suddenly I was holding Oberon Teag's arm in my hands, examining a bleeding gash that had laid skin and muscle well open. I found myself somehow back aboard the *Tatterdemalion*, a ship's doctor once more, and Teag sitting on the edge of my table, bleeding from a violent scuff with the one called The Albatross. I knew all of this without either of us having said a word...*because it had already happened months earlier.*

Teag grimaced as I gently laid his arm in his lap. "Aaa, fuckin' Aubrid, I'll gut him when he sleeps, the bastard."

One of the *loblolly* boys stepped through the partition, a plaster case in hand. "Your instruments, sir."

Was this a dream? Had I passed out from exhaustion in the jungle and now my mind entertained a delirium? Try as I may, I could not force myself to wake, could do nothing but watch and helplessly relive moments from the not-so distant past, a passive observer as if of a puppet show or play.

I saw myself put out my hand, accepting the case from the crewman. "You'll need to doff your tunic," I heard myself say, opening the box as the boy stepped away from the table, putting his back to the mast.

"Why?" Teag curled his lip.

I waved my hand at him. "You're covered in blood. I'll need to see if you've sustained any other wounds."

The man scowled, then his eyes flicked to the right. "Get out, boy."

I began to protest. "I need his assist—"

"Out!"

I peered across the cockpit at the hapless young fellow, gave a small exhalation through my nostrils—a sad bit of defiance, I know. "Fetch my salvatory, if you would."

"Sir." The boy whipped the partition aside and was gone.

"And sound off when ye return!" Teag yelled after him.

I gave the man a look of confusion, but he disregarded my stare. He grabbed at his tunic with his good arm and stopped. "Little help?"

I aided Teag in removing his soiled blooded shirt, pausing when I noted his back in the flickering lantern light. My perplexity must have been clear. Delineated on the man's back was a sizeable tattoo of a map.

"Doc, I know ye may think it odd, but if ye make mention of the ink on me back ta anyone, well, the sea's awful wide and deep...."

I hardly heard the familiar threat. It didn't hold the same weight, nor burden my soul with terrible chains as it had months ago.

Months ago. Yes....

Something quite odd was afoot. A strange sensation came over me. I gazed upon that map for a long moment, while Teag sat there, his back to me, unmoving. I stepped away, suddenly dizzy.

"I caught the nearest memory," I heard Katalin say, and just like that, I blinked and awoke, that hellish prison I'd endured upon Drake's skein-ship faded into the night. I found her looking at me, her expression unreadable. "I brought your past forward in your mind."

"You...you're...?" I stammered, eyes widening in sudden realization. There was no other explanation for what had just occurred. I realized now. *Skein.*

Katalin's slender hand was still against my face, warm now. "I'm not a skeinwielder, as such, if that's your worry. I'm not even an adept. I never understood what I am or why this happens. Usually I have no control over it at all, but sometimes I can make small things, *insignificant* things, I can..." She trailed off.

Her hand pulled away, but I took it in mine, not wanting to let go of her touch or lose this peculiar moment. I started to say something, but her gaze came back to me. She withdrew her hand.

"In a few seconds we'll be discovered," she said, then took my face in both her hands and touched her full lips to mine. My eyes closed, my mind reeled—they were softer than I imagined.

Katalin pulled away as Lieutenant Hensley's voice suddenly wrecked the moment: "Ah...um, pardon, Doctor, M'lady...but this is not the best, um...*milieu* for a...rendezvous, if ye please? We shouldn't stray here, 'specially at night."

I wasn't sure just how to respond, my mind still reeling. Fortunately, Katalin spoke: "Apologies, Lieutenant. This is all just too much for me and I sought comfort from the good doctor." She looked at me. "I apologize, Doctor, for throwing myself at you."

"Uhm...quite all right," I managed to murmur, more breathily than intended.

Katalin turned and strode quietly back to where the others were asleep. I watched her fade from the silvery moonlight into the gloomy silhouettes, then turned my gaze to the lieutenant. He stoically motioned for me to return, as well. I managed a small embarrassed smile and nod, and did as he suggested. I idly rubbed my lips with my fingertips, recalling the taste and feel of Katalin's kiss, waiting for slumber to unexpectedly wash over me.

The next morning arrived much too soon. I sat up and stretched, still fatigued and shivering from the dampness of my garb. My eyes roved to Katalin, who sat several spans distant, working the snarls from her hair. Then, as the chilly mist that pervaded the night gave way to another day of sweltering heat, I checked Captain Bellows. He yet lived, but seemed to have worsened further—if that were at all possible.

Meanwhile, Dominy alerted Lieutenant Hensley to something in the near distance: a narrow dirt track, but no mistaking it for anything other than a trail. Whose was the question, but after everyone had roused and Marshall and Dominy had built a litter for the captain from fallen branches, we decided to follow it.

After two, perhaps three, hours of walking, the heat of the day gradually fell heavy upon us, the air practically suffocating. More than once an eerie feeling caused my flesh to crawl, and I would pause to glance about, penetrating the understory as best I could for some horrible brooding thing watching us. I looked for the dark shapes of men, but made out nothing. The uncertain feelings refused to fade, however.

We continued along and the trail eventually tapered to a tenuous shadow, lost among the wild plants. I peered up at the avenue of blue sky above, narrowed to a mere slit, then turned my gaze to Hensley and Marshall as they bore the captain on their makeshift litter. Both men looked done in, first whispering to one another with grim stares, then raising their voices into growls. Arguing, no doubt, and I wondered if it regarded their clandestine exchange I'd overheard last night. Were they deciding to give in and seek out Thadieus Drake?

"Shh!" hissed Teag suddenly. "Listen."

Then we all heard it: the beckoning sound of rushing water, somewhere just ahead. We stepped lively, rushing down the trail. A shaded clearing opened up to a long, thin, white rivulet of waterfall, flanked on each side by even thinner, trickling falls. The effusion cascaded twelve spans into a green pool, creating a calm lagoon hemmed by large blooms of white and vermillion, then flowed onward, resuming its current some forty spans downstream.

Someone hooted and all at once we rushed down an escarpment of rock and large serpentine roots tangling and wending their way through the sediment. Being one of the first to emerge from the growth, I started when a dozen or more birds took wing mere yards away, launching from their baths in a sudden upsurge of cobalt-blue and brilliant turquoise.

At first, the water surprisingly stung with its coolness, but after the initial shock I splashed my face, neck, and arms, thankful for the relief from the scores of fly bites I'd endured. Indeed, I started considering immersing myself entirely when a shadow fell over me.

"Here, Doctor," said Master Dominy, reaching into his kerchief and producing a plump, green, teardrop-shaped fruit. He tossed it to me.

I caught and considered it briefly. "Fig, is it?"

"Trees full of 'em just over yon," he replied with a wave of his hand toward the jungle.

"You shouldn't be wandering away from the group, young master."

"I reckoned everyone could do with something to put in their bellies. Sorry, sir. Not meaning to make any perils for the crew, beg your pardon."

"No, I…no apologies. Just…it's best, I think, if we all stay within sight."

"Very well, sir."

I held up the fig and smiled. "Thank you."

The boy nodded and strode away to dole out his findings to the others. I watched him present his gatherings to Hamish, Teag, and

Hensley, and turned back to the water just in time to spy a ripple in the reddish algae where it was all drifted in layers along the pool's edge.

Boatswain Marshall kneeled quite near the movement, splashing water on his face. He paused and looked up, then I heard it, as well: an odd hissing noise that emanated from all around. Katalin's words came to mind, but too late. I opened my mouth to shout a warning to the boatswain, but the water erupted in a glittering shadow and a thing jettisoned forth, grabbing the man up.

The size of a large horse, armored in bumpy iridian plates from white to yellow to brown to orange, the beast seemed an arthropod of some sort akin to those studied during my first term at the Collegium. Its plated head bore a pair of hook-like legs—legs with which it held the screaming Marshall aloft. It scrabbled sidelong at the water's edge on a multitude of sharp appendages attached to its thoracic and abdominal segments. Mandibles and mouthparts snapped and scissored furiously in a terrifying din, conjuring in my mind the image of a thousand crows pecking against a single pane of glass.

The Albiyan sprang into action. He bellowed and brandished his claymore, leaping past me, landing with one foot in the pool and one foot out. Hamish hacked savagely at the giant crustacean-creature, but his blade glanced off its chitinous armor. The thing twisted and swayed, backing further into the water.

Marshall had been continuing to scream as he was tossed about, but all at once, with a grotesque cracking noise, he warped into a red nightmare. Blood and gore showered the Albiyan, yet he managed to shear off one of the creature's forelimbs before it submerged with what remained of Boatswain Marshall. In the water to his knees, Hamish took one last thrust at where he thought the beast might be lurking just beneath the surface. Stabbing nothing, he growled and spouted a litany of curses in his native tongue.

Meanwhile, I searched for Katalin and found her standing alone on a moss-covered rise. She met my horrified gaze with a sad one of her own.

Don't let the boatswain near the water...

"Where's bloody Teag?" Hamish rapped out fiercely. He rushed toward us, claymore in hand, and a feral gleam yet in his eyes.

Oberon Teag had evidently decided to make the most of Marshall's death by fleeing into the jungle.

"There." Katalin pointed. "He ran that way."

"Wait!" yelled Lieutenant Hensley, but the Albiyan was already dashing off into the trees. The first mate turned to me and said imploringly, "We can't abandon the captain," as if he thought I, too, was planning to give chase—which I most assuredly was not; though, I didn't relish staying near the monster in the lagoon either, lest it decided to surface again.

"No, of course not," I said, and strode over to where he and Dominy stood. I peered back at Katalin just as Hensley spoke again: "M'lady, please, come away from the water."

"As you please, Lieutenant," she said slowly.

"Gods, what was that...that *thing*?" asked Dominy, his eyes still wide with fright.

"Not for sure, lad," Hensley answered, "but I've seen the like years ago on the Galleon Coast; all kinds of giant crabs and insects and other mutations. No way for a man to go. Poor Marshall. It's no way at all. May he rest in the morning tide with his lady love."

We stood quietly for several long breaths, a sullen mist rising in the sweltering heat as the tropical forest darkened. I felt the eyes again, and soon a commotion in the jungle drew up our heads. Something moved toward us through the underbrush.

Katalin looked at the ground beneath long-lashed drooping lids. She reached out and took my hand. Her words came fraught with a menace that stole my next breath: "*They* are here."

A crowd of shadows moved in the jungle, and Hamish stepped into view at the fore, his taut, suffused face set in a grim mask. Behind him came Thadieus Drake, tall and wide-shouldered, a crimson bandanna tied beneath his cocked hat, the brim of which partially shaded his grizzled face, yet not quite enough to hide those protean eyes, sometimes blue, sometimes gray, sometimes green, always deep-set and beaming. A broadsword with a gold basket-hilt hung in a scroll-worked baldric at his waist, and two burgundy gold-chased pistols were housed in a cross belt over his ruffled silk tunic. He bore another pair of black silver-chased pistols, one cocked in each hand, pointing them at the Albiyan's broad back. Upon seeing us, his black-whiskered lips imparted a feral grin like that of a hungry leopard's. He swiveled one pistol in our direction.

"Ho, what fortune!" the pirate captain greeted us in his off-putting, self-possessed baritone. "Doubly so that we should renew our acquaintance, good Doctor." Then Drake smiled at Katalin. "Ah, an' a flower of womanhood, as well? Truly, the gods are fine."

He moved into the clearing, prodding Hamish ahead of him with a pistol barrel. The dimness of the jungle had grown thicker, the sky above no longer blue but the color of slate, gray and heavy. From the darkness of the undergrowth, more men came into view, some nine or ten of them, with Oberon Teag among their numbers. Pirates, they were, every steely eyed one, with metallic rings in their ears, noses, some even their lips, and armed to the teeth with blades and pistol butts of every sort, their very bearing threatening murder.

Alongside Teag strode Aubrid, the Albatross, lean and scarred, with a hooked beak for a nose, black cavernous eyes, and a brass-hilted cutlass shoved through an orange sash about his slim waist. His tangled mess of iodine-stained hair and unshorn cheeks framed an evil pockmarked face I'd come to fear, and his black gaze bored malignantly into mine.

"Sea Lord's salty balls on the queen's chin, yer a game lot, aye!" Drake proclaimed. "Ye must be Lieutenant Hensley, then? Bellows' first mate? Bugger me if ye didn't lead a fine chase, lad. Slippin' off ta land in all that smoke—crafty, aye." Drake moved in close as he continued, and we clumped together as he directed Hamish with a wave of his pistol to stand among us. "But the chase ever ends sooner than later. Appears ta ha' taken its toll on poor Bellows. Now, I'm of a mind to make an accord, if ye will. Wha' do ye say, Lieutenant?"

"An accord?"

"Aye, that's wha' I said."

"Of what sort?"

"We seek the same merchandise, do we not? I have a ship, ye have a map."

What ruse is this? I suddenly wondered. My gaze darted to Teag, who shifted his feet. I realized then that Drake didn't know. Teag had never told him about the actual map.

"I don't hav—" Hensley began to answer.

"Lieutenant," I interrupted, gripping the first mate by the elbow and giving it a hard—*desperate*—squeeze, thinking to myself a slim chance in hell was better than none at all. "It's our only option," I said to him, "for the lady, and the boy, if not for all of us. Please. We must make an accord."

Hensley paused to look at me. The implication of admitting we had no such map then dawned on him, and he gave a small nod. "Very well," he said, "but I'll have you know I memorized the way and burned the actual map."

"'Ee's lyin'," said Teag. "Troo 'is bloody teef."

"Belay, ye scab!" Aubrid cut in harshly, clutching at the grip of his cutlass. "I'll cut yer tongue if ye spill any more muck."

Teag frowned. Neither man had forgotten the bad blood between them—at least Teag hadn't, I reckoned, though little did I care.

"Before we begin, first, Captain Bellows needs tending," Hensley persisted, before Teag fouled up our last chance to live through the next few moments. "He's in a bad way, thanks to you. Doctor Mallory did what he could, but he needs further care. I suggest we transport him back—"

"Methinks we can tend ta yer captain easy enough," interjected Drake, having stalked up to stand over the unconscious Bellows. He pointed the pistol in his left hand at the inert captain and pulled the trigger. The weapon spat a puff of white smoke and the resounding blast echoed throughout the deep dark jungle, shaking leaves from the canopy. Small shadows howled and screeched as they scattered or took flight from the topmost branches.

"Now he's jus' dead weight," Drake looked at us with a black stare.

My blood ran cold. I stood dazed. I found myself holding Katalin's hand in a bone-crushing grip. In his febrile state, I could but pray that Bellows had been mercifully oblivious to his cruel fate.

"Murderer!" roared Hensley. His normally expressionless face purpled in rage. He rushed at Drake.

The pirate captain's right-hand pistol wheeled in the charging man's direction. "Perhaps ye'd care to join yer sorry captain, Lieutenant? Think again before ye take that next step, 'cause I can fair guarantee it'll be yer last. T'would be a shame for all o' us, no doubt, if indeed yer the only one who can find the loot."

Hensley stood stock still as two of Drake's cutthroats stepped forward and took hold of his arms. The first mate's furious gaze stabbed at the pirate captain with smoldering eyes. "Damn you, you devil," he snarled, his statement pursued by a murmur of thunder.

"Not the first time I've been called such, and worse. Doubtful the last. Disarm him," Drake commanded, scowling.

Aubrid strode over and relieved Hensley of his saber and also grabbed a knife from young Dominy's belt. He turned his smirk on Katalin. "I'll have ta search this 'un," he leered. "Weapons stowed in garters an' such."

"Stay yuir bloody hooks off'a the lady, you white-livered jackal," said a harsh voice. Hamish had spoken, taking a menacing step forward with an enviably reckless bravado. Several blades raised and halted him, as warm droplets began precipitating through the canopy.

"Or what, Albiyan?" Aubrid asked contemptuously, meeting Hamish's darkly pallid face with a resentful glare. "Yer threats 'r empty as a crone's teat."

A faint smile came over Aubrid's malevolent face as he returned his attentions to Katalin, his grin just another ugly scar among many.

The fear and tension of the past two days curdled inside of me, and I relented to some firm hands taking hold of my upper arms from behind, pulling me a step back.

Katalin met Aubrid's wicked gaze defiantly, raising her small white chin, while a multitude of rain droplets pelted down, splattering the leafy foliage. The pirate used the tip of his cutlass to lift the hem of her skirt, revealing part of her smooth white leg.

The pirates leered. One of them whistled, eliciting chuckles.

"Relish your last few moments, Myg Rothan," Katalin said, bestowing a crooked half-smile that never reached her eyes. "You'll not see another night."

Aubrid's grin faded. "Quit yer chatter, wench."

"You've terrorized, stolen, raped, and murdered your last, you abandoned whore's get, son of a sea dog, taking your vengeance on the world, and for what?" she said, eyes narrow with contempt. "Breathe it in, Myg Rothan. Your last few breaths. Suck the jungle air into your foul, black lungs."

Aubrid struck Katalin across the mouth with the back of his fist. She staggered, while an unexpected passion for violence roused up inside of me. Aubrid hefted his cutlass and advanced.

Brooking my typical sense of good judgment, I wrested away from the hands locked around my arms and stepped forward, placing myself between him and Katalin. I grabbed Aubrid's wrists. The Myg Rothan's hot eyes burned into mine with a how-dare-ye expression. He pulled his sword arm from my grip and took a backwards step, giving himself more space to deliver a mortal strike.

The warm rain descended in sheets as the treetops tossed and leaned above us. I tensed, steeling myself, reckoning my final moment had arrived, here in some unmapped jungle in a heavy rainfall. Not how I'd envisioned my demise, I supposed. In that last intake of breath, I saw my bones lying amidst the dark soil and leafy vegetation, claimed by the earth beneath my feet, picked clean, forgotten.

"Avast now, Aubrey!" rumbled Captain Drake. "Leave off the good doctor for a moment. He's a gentleman and, as such, protectin' the young lady's honor as a proper man should. Now, if'n ye want ta fight him, ye have ta do it proper-like. Is that not right, Doctor? A duel for privileges, says I!"

The pirates all grinned and hooted.

"I'm no duelist," I said, quite overcome by a conflicting muddle of incredulity and resignation.

"Ha! How unlike is a sword to a scalpel?" Drake grinned fiercely, still keeping a casual eye on the livid Hensley. "Both lots are a butcher's trade at any rate."

"We'll settle this matter, aye," Aubrid said. He leaned in at me, a savage grin on his scarred, ugly face. "Yer a dead man now."

"To the contrary," stated Katalin, presaging what happened next while touching her fingertips to her bloodied lips.

A horn-like blare heralded some sort of white arc that whirred from the shadows. It made a *thwip* noise as it smacked the back of

Aubrid's neck. His eyes widened, then quickly glazed. I managed to spy a thin bone-like spur no more than a hand's-breadth in length jutting from his flesh, just before he crumpled to the jungle floor.

Something whooshed mere inches from my face, so close I felt a puff of wind on my brow. I realized more wicked darts arced through the rain, followed immediately by large, leaping, howling shadows, and yet another hair-raising horn blast. A nearby pirate—mayhap the one who'd been grasping my arms—looked down at his own chest where three of the ivory darts suddenly appeared. He teetered headfirst, landing in a heap.

I heard rather than saw Drake's pistol *fwash* and pop, as the jungle erupted in a hell borne nightmare of fearful shapes and frenzied screams. A tide of enormous creatures surged out of the trees, something akin to hairless naked apes, their skin glistening wet, with powerfully molded limbs and large wide mouths filled with gnashing yellow teeth. If I thought Hamish a large man, these were indeed giants, easily a head taller than the Albiyan. They seemed to exude an intangible aura to me, of something primeval and savage and borne of the early depths of a time before history. I had read accounts of early men in my various studies, barbarians who roamed the lands in a time when the Dwarrow empires and the Phaderi houses spanned from Sunderlands to Darkelands. *Isaurians*, they are called, the evolution of man in stasis, classified just above the order of birds and beasts, pushed for long centuries into the wild places by the encroachment of one civilization after the next.

Are these such men? I wondered.

Katalin's hand found mine, or rather mine, hers. I drew her along in my steel grip as I dashed anywhere, as long as it was away from this fierce pandemonium where pirates and primitives clashed in a dark jungle storm.

I chanced a look over my shoulder to see Lieutenant Hensley, having recovered a blade, stab one of the massive Isaurians through the throat. The giant collapsed, wrenching the sword from his grasp, and others rushed *en masse* upon him. He roared as he fell beneath their onslaught. I saw, too, Aubrid and several others slung over shoulders, their limp forms borne away into the shadows and rain.

I rushed recklessly through the jungle downpour, pulling Katalin with me, as pistol blasts, screams, and barbaric howls split the darkness. We stumbled through the wet, twisted terrain for a hundred strides or more, around dozens of trees, through vines and branches, over fallen logs and brush, stopping just short of a sheer drop.

Katalin ran into me and I teetered precariously, drawing one ragged breath as I glanced down at a deadly fall. She pulled me by my tunic, and we both tumbled to the ground, me landing atop her.

We both lay still, facing one another in the gloom, sucking great gulps of air. Our eyes locked for a long moment as I became aware of her closeness, her face upturned mere inches from mine. I looked at her mashed lips, a smear of blood across her face, her auburn locks in disarray.

"Are you hurt?" I asked.

Her reply came unexpected. She responded with a kiss.

Katalin pulled my head down to her, fingers in my hair. We pressed firmly into each other, every part of me wanting her. Her wet lips opened and our tongues twined together as fiercely as our bodies. I kissed her narrow chin, down her jawline, until my lips and tongue found her neck, tasting her rain-wet skin, salty and sweet at once.

Katalin's head arched back. My left arm moved beneath her, supporting her and I glanced down, taking in the vision of this beautiful woman in the rain. Her eyes shut, full lips parted. My heart swelled in a way I couldn't fathom, nor did I care. I only wanted her, there and then, and didn't give a damnable fig where we were or how we'd come to be there.

Her upper body rose against mine, and my free hand ran up her side, across her ribs, stopping on her breast and remained there, kneading it through the cloth of her bodice. A soft moan escaped her lips that caused the blood in my extremities, most especially the male one, to thrum and go taut. I kissed across her collarbone, then the softer flesh above her breasts, silently cursed her clothing, wanting all of it off. I pulled her skirt, baring one shapely leg, grabbing her thigh and drawing it up. She wrapped it around me. Pulled my hips against her.

The erratic snapping of movement through the brush suddenly came from our right, shattering the moment, thrusting us back to our dilemma.

We looked up as Oberon Teag stumbled from the tree line mere spans away, nearly pitching over the same precipice. He panted and turned toward us, after a brief moment picking us out of the shadows with the horror-struck eyes of a man in flight.

Realization dawned on his features, only for a half-breath, then he flung up his arms and screamed for help as his pursuer, one of those naked giant savages, sprang from the jungle shadows.

The Isaurian grabbed Teag in its massive hands and heaved him up. I spied in Teag's hand a glint of metal, a long sliver, a dirk perhaps. He screamed unremittingly, kicking his legs and twisting his torso as he stabbed again and again into his assailant's neck and shoulders.

I lay aghast and gaping as the Isaurian uttered a bestial roar and squeezed with all its might. Teag ceased screaming and arched back, raising his pain-contorted face to the dark drizzling canopy. The dirk dropped from his fingers, and the giant gave a final wrenching motion, causing something inside of Oberon Teag—his vertebrae most likely—to make a loud sharp crack. The man's feet jerked spasmodically, then his entire body relaxed.

The damage wrought by Teag took its toll then. Its quarry now slain, the Isaurian wavered. Still holding the lifeless Teag in the crook of its elbow, the giant stepped clumsily to one side once, twice, and then enough for both of them to pitch over the cliff's edge.

After the span of no more than a breath or two, a grotesque *thwop* came up from the precipice. Katalin and I lay motionless, listening, slumped on our little wet mound of decayed earth. I know not how long we lay there, panting, but we spoke no more until I'd regained my wits. Still, I trembled, taking some little comfort in Katalin's presence as the gravity of our predicament pervaded my mind.

"We're doomed," I stated flatly.

A long moment passed in silence as the rain lessened.

"Yesterday," I continued, "you said I'd be there at the end, you, me, Dominy, Drake...is this what you meant?"

"No," she said, then paused so long I thought it to be her only reply. I looked at her profile, and could tell she was trying to make sense of something. "No...something else, something more...something terrible...and unforeseen. I cannot skein it. It's peculiar."

"Well, can you skein us off this bloody island?"

"No. I'm not like that. I only see things, and I don't have power over…" Her voice faded.

"Over what?"

She raised her long slender hand to shush me, then gave a subtle motion of her head. I turned to look where she indicated, spying two figures gliding through the dark. I feared the worst, that the savages had located us. Rather, I made out the taller of the two as Thadieus Drake, pulling along behind him the boy, Dominy, and bearing directly for us.

"I expect it rarely gets more inevitable than this," I said. "You certainly present a new view on the matter of one's destiny, m'lady. That, I have to admit."

We came to our feet as Drake strode up, gripping his red-stained broadsword in one hand, Dominy's skinny arm in the other. He pushed the boy at us and fixed me with a dark frown. It didn't escape my notice that three of his four pistols were missing, but the butt of one could be seen, the rest of it tucked in a dark sash around his waist.

"Ye don't want ta die, do ye, Doctor?" Drake softly asked.

I shook my head.

"Then best ye tell me the truth about the map. See, I reckon Hensley lied. No fool, am I. By hook or by crook I'd cut ta the heart of it, except now the bastard's dead as dead, and yer thankfully not, so I'm turning my attentions to ye. Too bad yer little gesture ta him was fairly noted. I'm not blind, either, y'see. So, let's hear it, Doctor. Where's that fine little map?"

It mattered little now whether I told Drake or not. I nodded. "Teag," I said. "He had it, though he's dead."

"Dead?"

"Slain by one of those...things. They pitched over the edge, just there," I responded, indicating the spot where the Isaurian had fallen with Teag's corpse. I noticed for the first time, some ways in the distance through the break in the jungle, a craggy tree-blanketed mountain rising up from a white mist. It radiated something menacing, causing me to shiver.

Drake spared a glance in the direction I'd pointed, and returned a narrow-eyed gaze to mine. "He had the map then, ye say?"

I nodded again. "Tattooed on his back," I answered.

"Poxy little bilge rat." The pirate pursed his lips and thought for a moment. As he did so I realized the rain had ceased. Wispy vapors steamed from the ground in the rising heat. "I didn't come all this way ta lose the treasure o'er a damnable cliff," he said, then waved his blade. "Come. We're goin' ta get that map."

I hesitated, then: "How so?"

"Yer expertise, my grit, and a strong vine rope," he answered smoothly.

"I don't see how we could possibly—"

Drake's brow lowered, and he pointed the tip of his bloodied sword at Katalin. "Evidently ye care fer the wench, so don't force me ta get ugly, Doctor. I've lost fair more than a dozen o' my crew ta this point on our little enterprise, so tryin' my patience right now is rather ill-advised."

"But more of those things are out there," I ventured.

"We risk that movin' forward 'r back. I'd quite prefer ta die strivin' fer a prize than tuckin' me tail and runnin' back gainin' fer naught."

So by virtue of his sword and reputation, Drake held us captive. We spent the next few hours collecting vines and twisting them to fashion a makeshift rope, while the pirate kept one eye on the jungle and the other guarded on us. At one point as Drake took his attention away, cutting vines, I located Teag's fallen dirk, casually swept it up and slipped it in my satchel.

"Good enough," said Drake, assessing the rope with a hard yank. He tossed the end to Dominy. "Knot it round the doctor, lad."

"Me?" I asked.

"Aye. Yer ta fetch the map."

"But, I can't carry him back up here!" I stammered.

"Bah! I care not for Teag's mangy carcass. Yer a chirurgeon so jus' ya bring us that map now, eh?"

I imagine I paled at that, sparing a worrisome glance over the ravine's edge. Below, I could see the two twisted forms of Teag and the Isaurian among the jagged rocks and a slithering ribbon of dark water. The sheer drop, though not as deep as I had imagined, was nonetheless fatal even if one's back were not broken or they had been stabbed numerous times.

"If I help you with this," I asked, "please do me just one thing."

"Ask," said Drake.

"Passage to the mainland...and if something should happen to me, your word that you'll deliver the lady and the boy to a safe berth, unmolested by your crew. We're at your mercy, Drake, but I'm asking just this one thing as my only recompense for helping you find this treasure."

"That's been my intent all along, Doctor." The pirate grinned through dark whiskers. "Ye have my word."

Despite the answer, I did not believe the man. I felt both panicked and angered, but rather than show it, I watched Dominy cinch the rope around my waist. The boy turned and looked at Drake. "He'll need my assistance. I should go with him."

"No!" It came out of my mouth more emphatically than intended. For some reason I wanted brave young Dominy to stay topside with Katalin. I couldn't stomach the thought of Drake being alone with her, even if her only companion was a young cabin boy.

"I'm sorry, Doctor," the boy murmured.

I gave him a small smile. "You're a good young man, Dominy. I wish I had just a measure of your courage."

"Alright now." Drake prodded us to silence, then instructed Dominy to tie the other end of the rope around a nearby tree, which he did, while Katalin looked at me and smiled somewhat with a certitude that spoke: *Take heart. Remember what I have told you.*

I nodded wordlessly, relying on her prophetic talent, as well as the tensile strength of our primitive rope, to hold true. Drake ordered Dominy and Katalin to take hold of it as I leaned a bit for leverage. I drew a long breath, and then lowered myself backward into the verge.

The rope gave some length at first, and I held my breath as I plummeted into space for a brief moment, but then my feet struck the precipice wall. The crude tether creaked ominously, but held firm. I steadied myself. The descent, though nerve-wracking, went quicker than I anticipated.

I touched the ravine floor a mere two spans from the Isaurian's broken body where it lay with its legs half-submerged in the gurgling black stream. The giant's head twisted at an extreme angle, its large maw gaping open in a silent bellow, two cold black eyes seemingly watching my approach. I assumed it dead, but gave as wide a berth as I could, while nonetheless scrutinizing it. Naked and sun-bronzed, in addition to the nine or ten fresh stab wounds in its broad and once-powerful shoulders, the Isaurian's muscular body bore a myriad of scars, some of which appeared ceremonial. Black and gold war paint decorated its wide-boned face, and a large conch shell lay beside the massive head, having once apparently hung from the giant's neck on a tattered cord. I surmised this as the source of the earlier horn blasts, and attributed this particular Isaurian as a leader among its people.

Though brutish and heavy-browed, in truth the giant appeared quite man-like. I suddenly felt the long lost ages of a primeval world come over me, when such men as these, wild and vital, marched out of the mists of time in an age of ice and fire and asserted their dominion among the elder races. But now, from what I understood, the age of the Isaurians had faded, and they receded into the dark places of the world from whence they had come, little more than painted primitives and savage man-eating marauders.

I looked beyond the Isaurian at Teag's shattered body. Though I'd known the man, and rarely felt even small pity for him, to see his corpse dashed face down upon the rocks, his lifeblood cooled in a seeping puddle, I breathed a silent prayer for his misguided soul. It was more than I would give for Aubrid, wondering if even now his body were being flensed and carved to fill Isaurian bellies.

With a somber countenance, I removed my satchel and set about the grisly task of skinning Oberon Teag.

Perhaps an hour later, I clambered over the cliff's edge and exhaustedly presented to Drake a bloody parchment. He looked at it briefly, stressing displeasure in its legibility. I began to explain the effects of saturation, but he waved me off with a curse.

After a few moments of silence, Drake flourished his sword at us and we set off in the shimmering heat, back into the rank jungle. After an hour or more we came into an expanse of thorny understory. We pulled our way through it, the long needle-like barbs snagging clothes and flesh.

"Ow!" hissed Dominy from just a few spans behind. I turned as he lifted up his right foot and plucked out a needle. It hadn't occurred to me that the lad wore nothing on his feet. They were a mess of raw flesh and dozens of small cuts.

I walked back to him in my knee-high Pendaran leather boots. "Here, let's get you through this, young Master."

"What's that, Doctor?" he asked. I could tell he wanted to be brave and cause no bother, but his lip quivered and tears formed in the corners of his eyes.

"Up with you," I said, and turned my shoulder so he could clamber onto my back. He paused. "Come on," I urged him. "It's alright, young master. Let's just get you through these blasted thorns now. Up. Besides, I never thanked you for the fig."

I'm no large man, but as far as doctors go, I'm rather fit. Besides that, I hail from good stock, as my father and brothers are all strapping men, none of us slouches, and tending more to a rangy physique—me, of course, the runt of the litter. Mallory men made good soldiers and athletes and, for the nonce, good creatures of burden, as I hefted Dominy up onto my back.

"Move it, ye laggards!" Drake glared back at us.

After the days of hard travel, fear, and my travails in the ravine, fatigue clutched at me vigorously. Dominy wasn't heavy for a lad his age, perhaps no more than eight stone, but the uneven slope and patches of soft clumpy soil did little to relieve the matter. I staggered sideways into the bushes more than once, wicked barbs prickling my legs and forearms and, by the time we were midway through the patch, I was already covered with dozens of stinging welts and punctures, beginning to wonder if I'd made a wise gesture.

"What happened to your shoes?" I asked to take my mind from my misery.

"Oh, I ain't had shoes in my life, sir."

"Well, what do you do when it's cold out, during the Brooding season?"

"If it gets too cold, I wrap them in wool or some such. We had a patched up pair some man from the church gave us, but my brother, he got them. My feets are tough as leather though, sir."

Another reminder of my cosseted life. To most, a pair of decent shoes was more than an afterthought. Back home, I had a wardrobe full. "I have no doubt they are," I said, wishing I'd had the kindness to donate my footwear to the local abbey before embarking to the Collegium.

Suddenly, the trees thinned and the jungle opened up at the base of the ominous mountain. Drake halted us and peered at the map, and I eased Dominy to his feet.

From where he stood in the shadowy arch of the clearing's wooded entrance, the pirate captain turned to us and smiled. "I believe we have arrived," he said.

We warily advanced into the open. Ahead of us, the lowering sun tinted the sky a sickly yellow as it descended toward the mountain, while the thunderheads of the day's earlier storm darkened the entire horizon to our right.

Here we observed the first signs of habitation on the island other than the brutish savages; though the mysterious inhabitants had evidently departed long since. Twin rows of peculiar five-foot-high *stelae*, a half-dozen each to a side, roughened and carved with hundreds of worn sigils, flanked an overgrown pathway leading into the open. The ravages of time and jungle had taken their toll on this place. Once several stone structures had filled the clearing; these now existed as little more than piles of rubble, hemmed in by a crude wall of mud and stone mostly overtaken by low vegetation and thorny scrub. Directly ahead some eighty spans distant, a ziggurat in moderate repair somehow held off the jungle's grasp, holding silent dominion over the remains of an eerie, lost world.

"Ha! There we are," said Drake triumphantly, holding up the gruesome skin map, the tracings of the temple barely evident upon it. He gave an appraising look to the structure. "'Tis the only useful thing ye e'er done did, ol' Teagy."

"I feel so much death," Katalin whispered, moving close alongside me. "It's overwhelming."

"Drake, I don't like this," I said, taking Katalin's hand in mine. "Something's wrong here."

"Nay," the pirate captain replied. "There be somethin' here, aye, but...it calls out." He paused as if listening for something, cocking his head slightly. "D'ye hear it?" He turned to look at us, a strange, covetous gleam in his eyes. "I hear it. Come."

When we paused, he sneered. He plucked the pistol from his sash, cocked it, and motioned with it toward the ziggurat. I sighed and relented, looking at Katalin and Dominy before striding past Drake and down the path amid the stelae. The rest followed and we picked our way precariously through the ruins. I feared something would lunge at us any moment, but soon enough the temple loomed large, its obscure carvings barely legible upon the decaying stonework. We stood at the base of a score of steps leading up to an entryway framed with carven lintels. Above it hung a moldering skeleton, limbs splayed, grinning skull face warning us off.

The muzzle of Drake's pistol prodded the back of my neck. Mouth dry, unable to swallow, I ascended the crumbly steps, the others in my wake, to the gaping entryway. Six niches to each side were inset with ancient skulls, the brow of each displaying the faint evidence of a *runemark*, doubtless some terrible curse or other ward of nefarious power.

"Captain, please—" I hesitated, feeling such dread in my heart it was nearly beating from my chest. My hair bristled at the thought of going into that forbidding-looking temple. If I had felt fear to this point, I knew not what sort of primal terror now had me in its grasp.

"Oh ho, Captain now, am I?" said Drake; yet, this came without his usual barbed tone. Even so, the muzzle prodded me forward. "Go," he hissed.

"But how are we to see?" I asked.

As if something had overheard my query, a pale luminescence emanated from the temple's depths. It did not flicker as fire did, but rather emitted a barely discernable aurulent glow; *skeinlight* I assumed.

Drake poked me with his pistol again, urging me on, so I strode warily between the lintels, beneath the grinning skeleton, and into the forbidding temple. My eyes were forced to adjust to the dark, finding the skeinlight's source still a ways off so that the passageway was but vaguely alight. Countless strands swept across my face and I turned my head, wiping away the sticky filaments. Drake kept prodding at me, and I used my hands to paw at the cobwebs, gritting my teeth and wordlessly moving forward.

Silently we went, feet scraping the stone floor, until we came to a small musty chamber at the bottom of some eroded steps. Skeinlight dimly lit the room from no apparent source, granting enough illumination for us to see murals all along the walls depicting rituals, domestic scenes, battles, and human sacrifices. Though faded, I found myself awed by what I could see, both by the meticulous brilliance and the immediate spectacle of glimpsing life in some court long-lost in the passage of time.

"Keep going," hissed Drake.

So I led on, moving through a brief passageway into yet another mural-decorated chamber roughly the same size as the first, but with a high roof that could not be seen and a choice of three passages: left, right, and straight ahead. A question froze on my lips when the golden light from the middle archway pulsed.

I gulped.

"That's it," Drake's breathy voice had turned husky. "That's the one. D'ye hear? That voice?" He looked at us, eyes agleam with a feral light like that of a ravenous wolf.

I shook my head, just barely.

He scowled and looked at the others, Katalin with her hand laid softly on Dominy's shoulder. They, too, responded quietly in the negative.

"How can ye not?" His voice reverberated in the chamber. "Bah! Go on then. Forward!" He gestured with his pistol at the central passage.

Though I would never accuse Drake of being the sanest man I knew, he seemed on the verge of sheer madness. I felt the need to draw him away from this recklessness and uttered the first thing that came to mind: "If the treasure lies beyond," I said, "you promised safe passage..."

Drake's arm outstretched, his pistol aimed at me, a fiendish look of purpose on his face. "Go," he said with an angry-looking sneer.

I moved into the archway straight ahead, fearful over many things, the integrity of a murdering pirate's word of honor foremost among them.

As I proceeded, I fought the need to fetch Teag's dirk from my satchel, suddenly thinking the only chance for the three of us lay in my ability to surprise the man and deliver a killing strike. But such a desperate lunge…and the pirate's twitchy trigger finger…it seemed unlikely.

Cowardice clutched hold of me, drawing me into a wretched state of inaction in which I could only shuffle forward. I reasoned consolingly with myself. Even if I did succeed in killing Drake, the matter of an inescapable island-full of giant cannibals seemed a bit of a challenge. The *Tatterdemalion* was our only real chance. For that reason, if none at all, Drake needed to live.

In the midst of my inner flurry of doubt and indecision, we entered a large square chamber alight in a golden glow. Four pockmarked columns stretched into the oppressive darkness high above us. Beyond the nearest, I could see a shallow pit in the room's center, hemmed by obelisks little more than an arm-span tall and incised with whorl-shaped, pulsating sigils. Something small and orb-like lay atop a blocky granite pedestal in the center of the depression. The short hairs on my neck bristled as I took a few more leery steps, the others moving slowly behind me, for the obelisks projected beams of light directly at the orb, and I saw it for what it was: a cryptic, rune-covered skull.

We stood, the four of us, at the edge of the steps that led down into the pit. At first I thought it a trick of the light, how the orbital cavities seemed to radiate, then realized the eyes were actually crystallized golden orbs. This decorative ornament must have been the skull of a great king, or perhaps a deity of some sort.

Nio lurium vo su, sangre mih sangre, a foreign voice rasped unto our ears. In a dialect both strange yet familiar, the words became plain in my mind: *A new day's light upon you, blood of my blood.*

Katalin, Dominy, and I glanced about, confused and looking for the source of that croaking voice.

"We've come fer a great treasure," Drake called out. "Reveal yerself and guide us ta what we seek."

Qua su atis? A treasure you seek, do you?

A small silence followed. I watched Drake as he peered about the chamber, eyes wild, tongue nervously licking his bottom lip, and then a shuffling noise drew all our gazes toward the skull-topped pedestal. A figure entered the far side of the depression, draped in an ankle-length sleeveless white vestment, open down the middle and trimmed with gold. Beneath it the figure wore a plain black cassock; over it a black hooded mantle from which flowed a long snowy beard.

"Many might call it as such," said he, with a hoary voice that sounded weak and ghostly, yet in my mind suggested profound strength deep within. "But what is housed in this place—this long forgotten temple—is meant for the proper heir. Only they who may prove it through lineage are welcome here."

The figure had spoken as he moved to the pedestal and stood beside it. He reached up and drew back his black hood to reveal a gaunt face illumined by skeinlight rays, pale and wrinkled, and a balding head of hair to match his white beard. Most striking, however: his eyes. The man fixed us with a pupil-less gaze, displaying orbs of pure gold behind his lids, a perfect glimmering imitation of the skull on the pedestal to his right.

"Lineage? What lineage?" demanded Drake, eyes narrowed and lip well curled.

The man turned toward him. "The bloodline of Tisarian, of course. My *heir*."

"I'm not 'ere ta submit to a gods-damned bloodline. Where's the treasure, old man? I've lost all patience so ye'd best answer quickly 'r else I—"

A long finger stabbed at Thadieus Drake and halted him mid-sentence. "You have a rude manner about you. I like it not," said the golden-eyed man, a frown on his wizened face. "You're one who likes to hear himself talk, I can tell."

Drake stiffened, standing awkwardly erect, seemingly frozen in place.

"What of the rest of you?" The man turned and squinted at us. "Have you lost all patience, as well?"

In the gleam of those eyes it seemed to me that something very powerful roused. A long uncomfortable moment passed as something palpable hummed in the air. My flesh crawled in spite of myself.

Katalin took a step forward. "You are Tisarian the Skeinborn? Bringer of Light to the Darkelands, Lord of the Crystal Arch, who, in the presence of Avin the Prophet, ascended to become the Walking God?"

"Ah, Avin…" The man's countenance lightened. "Long has it been since I have known the Grace and Light of his company." He looked at Katalin, scrutinizing her. "You know of me. Can it be?" His eyes narrowed at her, and they flashed with an odd light, but then he frowned and shook his head. "Ah, no."

The man Katalin called Tisarian turned and looked at me. Subtle warmth coursed through my body. He shook his head slightly, his coruscating gaze moving on to Dominy for a brief moment, then finally on the motionless Drake, who relaxed, able to move again. He stepped back, glowering.

"You? You're my heir?" Tisarian looked outwardly dismayed, but he recovered quickly. His tangled brow lowered. "A murderous, Drear-tainted whore's get?" He scratched his bearded chin, then sighed. "Why am I not surprised?"

Tisarian might not have been surprised, but I was more than a bit dismayed. Our paths had led us to this one destination, some forgotten ruin on a forgotten island, and here we stood in the presence of a spectral skeinwielder, some legendary figure from centuries agone, who'd just acknowledged Thadieus Drake as his bloody heir? I smothered my need for a raging bout of nervous, incredulous laughter.

"Here is my vessel." Tisarian gestured at the skull on the pedestal. It rose into the air, emitting a faint glow. "It's my skull, in fact, which is a bit odd to look at, I admit. Especially if you're me…" Tisarian shook his head, broke himself from sinking into a mire of distracted reflection, I supposed. "It holds a measure of my essence, bestowing whoever claims it access to great knowledge of the skein. I have waited…I know not how long…" He peered at me. "What year is it?"

"2142," I said.

His brows raised, but it was hard for me to tell surprise in those golden orbs. "Ascendant?"

"Uh, Keeper's Age."

"Ah. Reckoning of the Drunelords. I see. I almost thought it had been nearly two-thousand years. Not that it matters now, in the Beyondtime...where was I?"

"You've waited long...?"

"Yes. I have waited long for one of my forebears to be drawn here through an ages-old *ges*. Over three-hundred years, I approximate." His bushy brows lowered, giving a sudden dark look. "And it's with some disappointment that you have proven unworthy of this favor. Now, rather, I must take measure of these others in your company and decide who to gift with this great power."

Drake cursed. "No," he snarled. "If ye speak truth, this is my birthright. I won't have it denied me!"

Tisarian's eyes narrowed, his voice dropping low. "You believe the choice is yours, do you?"

The next few moments went by slowly, and I stood rooted. Stupefied, it seemed. The pirate captain ignored Tisarian's ghost, stalked forward and lunged to grab the hovering skull. Katalin swept past me, her soiled and tattered dress swishing. She snatched Drake's tunic at the shoulder, tried to pull him away. And then my blood went cold as Drake whirled on her, yanking his arm away, madness a'gleam in his eyes. A lone pistol shot clamored in the confines of the chamber. Wreathed in a plume of white smoke, Katalin dropped to the floor.

My vision ran red. *"Nooo!"* I screamed, puzzled in my haze to find it accompanied by some deep bellow from the steps to my right.

Something large leapt from behind a column. A few desperate blinks later I realized it was the Albiyan, Hamish, stripped to the waist, covered in mud and blood. Seemingly having followed us and hidden behind a pillar, he now pounced like some ferocious tiger leaping at its prey. He charged Drake with all speed, gave a great sweep of his blade.

The pirate captain barely managed to spring away, his tunic the worse for wear with an open slash through the side. Drake's broadsword hissed from its scabbard, and both he and Hamish looked fiercely into the eyes of the other. The tall men circled, blades bared, while the hovering skull emitted intense rays of light in every direction, causing their silhouettes to play about the chamber as if a score of men or more had arrived to give battle.

Dominy hunched over Katalin, worry and fright etched on his pale face. Tisarian seemed to have vanished, but I gave him little thought. In my satchel, my fingers wrapped about the grip of Oberon Teag's dirk. I glared at Drake as he and Hamish advanced and gave ground to one another. Rage seethed within my breast. I wanted desperately to strike at him. If I could but flank him to offset the Albiyan's pressing attacks...but I shook, as if from a sudden chill.

My gaze turned to Katalin. Her face, bathed in the golden light from the floating skull, grimaced. *She yet lived.* I had presumed her dead, my ire so fixed on attacking the pirate, but without another moment's thought I released the knife and rushed to her side. My rage diminished as Thadieus Drake fled my mind, filling up instead with desperate concern for this mysterious, beautiful—and *dying*—woman.

Kneeling beside her, I could see she was in shock. I instructed Dominy to lay Katalin's head in his lap and positioned her on her back, then fished my toolkit from my satchel. I unrolled it and retrieved my scissors, using them to cut her tattered bodice and blouse to reveal a gaping, blood-leaking wound roughly the size of a Berdainese penny in her abdomen just left of her umbilicus. I rubbed my fingers across her flat belly, feeling for anything out of the ordinary, examined her sides and back for an exit wound. Finding nothing, I steeled myself and reached for my scalpel. The ball was inside.

"Doctor," breathed Katalin, suddenly roused. She looked at me through glazed eyes. Fear knotted inside my chest. "Don't make a...fuss," she said weakly. "It is...meant to be. I have foreseen it. You mustn't—"

"Shush now, m'lady. Save your strength."

The struggle between Drake and Hamish moved dangerously close, and Dominy flinched at the grating of steel as a shower of sparks fell over us. Past Dominy I could see Drake grin and lunge at Hamish, but the Albiyan deflected the broadsword and returned a lightning-quick slash aimed at the pirate captain's head. Drake danced away, thrust low at his enemy's groin, barely missing by a hair's breadth. This happened in the blink of an eye it seemed, a ferocious bear against a lean, darting wolf.

"Steady on," I urged Dominy. "Time's of the essence. Let's help the lady. The Albiyan will deal with Drake."

The boy nodded. "Yes, sir."

Katalin winced and coughed as Dominy gently stroked her hair away from her ashen brow.

"I'm sorry, m'lady," I said to her, "but I fear you're bleeding inside. I have to look and see what damage you've taken."

She shook her head slowly, a gesture of defeat. "It's no use...the skein shows all. My hour is...upon me. I've seen it...."

"I can't believe that, m'lady. I won't. You've predicted rightly since yesterday, I'll give you that, but I won't sit here and let you die, not as long as I can do something. Now, please?" I looked at her, imploring.

She coughed again, weakly, licked her lips as if to say something; instead, her eyes rolled back and she shuddered. Katalin's head lolled in Dominy's lap.

My stomach dropped. I cursed.

"Doctor?" the boy said anxiously.

"Here, put this between her teeth." I handed Dominy a small strip of leather, then some rags. "When I tell you, use these to wipe away the blood so I can see what I'm doing."

He did as I asked, saying, "Yes, sir. I've assisted on board before, sir."

"Good lad," I replied as I gripped my scalpel.

It can be difficult to know where to cut when blood pools in the abdomen, so I took a deep breath, then pressed the blade to Katalin's smooth white skin no more than a thumb's length above the wound. As I made the incision, dark blood immediately seeped through, and a slight buzzing noise hummed in my ears. The golden light in the chamber brightened.

I nodded for Dominy to wipe the blood away.

Hot sweat ran down my back beneath my tunic as I continued cutting through the layers of fat and abdominal membranes. *Here is the true test,* I thought, as the humming in the chamber reverberated and, in the depths of my mind, I swore I heard choral voices, but the roar and fury of battle assaulted me, drowning the voices out. My scalpel sliced cleanly through the serous membrane and, as anticipated, blood geysered upward.

Dominy used what was left of the rags to stem the flow, even frantically removing his tunic and using it, but I swallowed hard as I noticed Katalin's small bowel, the *eileos*, had been shredded.

"No..." I pawed through the segments, but could find no way to mend the damage. "She was right." I wiped sweat from my brow with a blood-spattered forearm. "There's nothing I—"

Katalin's mouth was half open, her head dropped.

Dominy looked at me. "Keep going, sir! You must try...."

"I...I can't," I said, unable to meet the boy's desperate gaze. "There's nothing I can do." My throat felt parched. I couldn't swallow. My gaze swept over Katalin and I became utterly heartsick, completely lost and alone as I'd never been.

Though the men still fought within the chamber, the ringing of their combat sounded dull and distant.

Dominy must have realized how deflated I felt. We regarded one another over Katalin's body, drenched in her blood. The boy gave me a small nod, imparting to me whatever comfort a shoeless, shirtless cabin boy could.

I looked sideways at Teag's knife on the stone floor, felt my own mouth curl up, anger welling up once more.

Golden light shined from overhead, causing Dominy and I to squint up. The sigil-etched skull floated a mere arm-span above us, terete-shaped motes of bright light eddied about it, tracing argent patterns in the air.

"I lost many a friend in my day. Many a friend," said Tisarian's ghost, suddenly standing behind Dominy. He placed a semi-translucent hand on the boy's shoulder. His golden-eyes seemed oddly forlorn. "My greatest friend, he was a brother to me in all things but blood...the black tip of a *drakhölve* arrow festered in his guts for days. He was a strong man, the strongest I ever knew. I arrived late, but he had already passed. The skein is strong in me, but no measure of skein can return a man's soul, nor would I have. He was one with the Light."

The man blinked, returning to the moment. "I've decided on the boy. I had wished to pass it on within my bloodline..." He paused to glance at Thadieus Drake, who was in the midst of a lunge at the Albiyan. Both men were bloodied.

Tisarian shook his head. "Alas. Then, I intended to bestow it on the woman, her being skein-touched, but the boy will do. A halo surrounds you," he said, nodding his head at me. "You're much too trussed in the bonds of your science. The boy has skein blood, very mild. Mind you, his abilities must be culled and tempered. Heed that, else he'll soon go mad—"

"Pardon me, m'lord," I interrupted, "but Lady Katalin told me her fate was to die here and now. If you pass on your power—"

"A measure."

"A measure, then. But even with that, can we save her?"

"Her essence ebbs. It is moving from this world...but I suppose I could guide him."

"Begging your pardon then, but can we get on with it?"

"Indeed," he replied, speaking softly. "Are you willing, boy?"

I looked at Dominy, urging his response with a desperate gaze. He glanced down at Katalin, glanced up at the man, and quietly nodded.

"Be it so," the man said and placed his long, withered hands on the sides of Dominy's head. The glowing skull moved slowly through the air until it transposed with the man's head. Merged together as one, the skull imbued the ancient man with a rictus grin, the sigils blazing into his flesh, which seemed to slough away from the bones of his face. The missiles of light accelerated frantically above us.

Across the chamber, Drake shouted at us, breaking from combat. He charged at Tisarian, Hamish hard on his heels.

"Put your hand into the woman's wound, draw the foreign metal to you, and will her body mended," Tisarian instructed.

I held her flesh taut as Dominy put his thin right hand into Katalin's abdominal cavity.

Curia vitalasae, the words echoed in my mind. *Curia vitae.*

"Curia vitalasae," Dominy whispered.

Drake raised his broadsword to strike just as the motes of light converged into a spiraling, blinding sphere. The entire chamber vanished. A loud crackle hummed. I felt strangely weightless for a brief moment, then a deafening chorus of countless voices rose from low to high in every range and pitch. Intense heat blasted at me from Tisarian's direction, or so I perceived. I shielded my face, squinting to see an arc of white skeinlight transfixing Dominy, outlining his body in a nimbus of shimmering gold.

"Take away your hand, boy!"

Dominy did so, and the chamber fell silent, as if the stone lid of a sarcophagus had slammed shut.

I blinked into the gloom, then watched, stunned, as Katalin gasped for air. Her body arced upward, and I grabbed at her, pulling her to me, feeling her warm breath on my neck. In awe I stared past her tangled mess of hair at the shadowy figure of Dominy. The boy returned my gaze through staring eyes of gold.

"That is...quite interesting," murmured Tisarian. I peered up at him; he, after inspecting Dominy for the span of a breath or two, dissolved, garb and all, into dust.

A long moment passed as the chamber darkened. I heard more than saw the *plink* of Dominy dropping the lead shot to the stony floor as, with Tisarian's absence, the skeinlight continued to fade.

I was feeling for Katalin's pulse in her neck as a shadow loomed over us. I glanced up to see Hamish. In one hand his naked blade glimmered dully, the other gripped the severed head of Thadieus Drake. He nodded down at me. "I should think we'll want ta be leavin' this hole," he said. "But first..." The Albiyan strode over to the pedestal that had previously displayed the skull of Tisarian and unceremoniously plunked down the head of the wizard-priest's disdained forebear.

"Thair's yuir bloody prize," Hamish remarked. He then crossed in the dark toward the pirate's fallen body, mere spans away from where Dominy and I knelt with the unconscious but steadily breathing Katalin. He bent and took up a selection of Drake's accoutrements: cocked hat; black pistol, cross belt, bejeweled rings of gold and silver, and ornate broadsword. He placed the hat on his head, draped the belt over his broad naked shoulder, then said, "Dark's comin' fast in here. Let's be away."

I stood, hefted Katalin in my arms. "Dominy?" I looked to the boy.

Could he even see with those cryptic eyes? As if he'd heard me, his next utterance imparted an answer somewhat. "It's...peculiar...my vision is changed...light or dark, it doesn't appear to mean anything...." He reached out and grabbed my toolkit, placed it in my open satchel, and gathered it all up. He stood and nodded to me in the dimness, as the obelisks faded completely. "I can lead," he said. "Follow me." And we strode quickly from the temple, behind Dominy's vague shadow.

Once outside, the three of us paused at the top of the steps, transfixed each in our own thoughts. I surveyed the spread of ruins throughout the clearing. The moon rode high and I could see some leagues beyond the treetops where the sea stretched toward the Orange Coast, toward the mainland, toward Dal Raedia, Anturia, and Berdain.

Katalin moaned and stirred in my arms, but did not waken. Under moonlight I could see that even the marks left by Aubrid's fist were absent. Her face was pristine, relaxed, and as lovely as ever.

"I can carry the lady, Doctor," said Hamish.

But I was not quite ready to relinquish her. "Not yet," said I, and the Albiyan nodded in understanding.

"Where will we go?" Dominy's gold eyes glimmered in the moonlight. He seemed rapt with everything around him, and I watched intensely this bone-thin youthful inheritor of so much power. Tisarian's treasure had been sought by so many, yet an unlikely cabin boy unwittingly found it. I wondered what would become of him. The skein exacted a heavy cost. It was well-known that certain guilds hunted unvarnished skeinwielders in order to guide them, but mostly as a safeguard, seeking them out to eliminate a threat before it inflicted undue damage.

"I lost a ship once, and now Drake's be mine by right o' combat. I say let's make it known." So said Hamish—now *Captain* Hamish— and truthfully enough.

I wordlessly swept my gaze to the grim set on his strong face, whose keen blue eyes burned a path through the jungle. He rested his large hand on the pommel of Drake's broadsword, and I imagined he fixed his sights somewhere down along the island coast where the

Tatterdemalion and her crew unsuspectingly awaited us. That was Hamish's treasure: mastery over his own ship once again. A sea brigand's ship, of course, under the precepts of a pirate's code, yet I had a feeling the man was eager for it.

Katalin. What was her treasure? Another chance at life, I suppose, bearing with her the knowledge that the Fates could be defied after all. Though, of course, that came by means of a legendary wizard-priest-turned-god, or at least some quixotic manifestation thereof, and for what end? I could not say; perhaps as a guide to Dominy along the skein path? T'was the only guess I envisaged. Perchance if that were her treasure, I daresay I could imagine better...and worse, to be sure. At least she lived.

Mayhap that was my treasure. A chance to connect to someone. It was long since I had deigned to care for anyone but myself. Disavowed by my family for my decision to study medicine, I spent the next eight friendless years in a large city at an establishment rife with academic rivalry. Whatever belief in humanity, whatever innocence I had left—no, make that arrogance—was robbed mere weeks upon my embarkation from Nantyrr, taken by Thadieus Drake in those miserable months pressed into his dark service.

Katalin was my treasure. That's what Tisarian had given me. I shifted her weight and held her tight, then followed Dominy and Hamish down the temple steps. The lad may have received Tisarian's treasure directly, but his favor rested upon the four of us in a variety of ways.

A new man departed those dark ruins under faint moonlight, trailing behind Dominy and his new eyes. Somewhere among those broken stones and cryptic stelae, the hitherto Doctor Alexandre Mallory remained. A renewed Mallory entered the jungle, embarking with the thought that none of us left unchanged. In our own way, we had all found Tisarian's treasure.

THANK YOU FOR BUYING MY BOOK!

That's bold and in all caps because that's just how thankful I truly am. Your support of my writing means more than you know, and I appreciate each and every visitor who spends a little of their time gracing the worlds I create. If you enjoyed *Tisarian's Treasure*, please leave a review on whatever site you purchased it to help spread the word. More reviews translate to more sales, and that, my friend, translates to more writing.

In case you're interested, my other writing credits include the fan-favorite *Legendlore* comic series for Caliber Comics, Iron Kingdoms and Warmachine RPG supplements for Privateer Press, and short stories in Fantasist Enterprise's *Sails & Sorcery: Tales of Nautical Fantasy*, Pill Hill Press' *Dark Heroes* anthology, and Rogue Blade Entertainment's *Assassins: A Clash of Steel Anthology*, all set in the world of Khaladune, where *Tisarian's Treasure* takes place. A more complete bibliography is available on Goodreads or on my blog (links below).

I'm currently working on several full-length fantasy novels in the world of Khaladune, and I'd love to hear from you. Yes, you! Encouragement definitely keeps me rolling along. Thanks again!

Connect with J.M. Martin

Goodreads: http://www.goodreads.com/jmmartin
Blog: http://ranting-and-raven.blogspot.com
Twitter: http://twitter.com/#!/martinjm70

Connect with Julie Dillon

Artist Julie Dillon did the wonderful artwork appearing herein, as well as all art and the cover of the original publication, *Sails & Sorcery: Tales of Nautical Fantasy*. See her online at http://www.juliedillonart.com and at http://jdillon82.deviantart.com.

Connect with Peter Ortiz

Peter is a rising cover artist whose digital paintings depict a wide range of dark emotion and edgy fantasy. Visit him online and see more of his work at http://standalone-complex.deviantart.com.

CPSIA information can be obtained at www.ICGtesting.com
Printed in the USA
LVOW08s0253200814

399907LV00001B/78/P

9 781466 255388